C000213181

Let Me Be

....

Mariem Ushe

Copyright © 2022 by Mariem Ushe

All rights reserved.

No portion of this book may be reproduced in any form without written permission from the publisher or author, except as permitted by U.S. copyright law.

Contents

Let Me Be

~ ~~

"How can you prove whether at this moment we are sleeping, and all our thoughts are a dream; or whether we are awake, and talking to one another in the waking state?"

- Plato

~~~

1: Open Wide

B urnt almonds. The rancid stench hummed around in my nose in the most offensive way, lingering and forcing my eyes open.

Glancing around the stark white room, I searched for the cause of the smell. The bright lights reflected off of the clean, white walls and it took a few seconds for my eyes to adjust, only to see the large machines and their systems projecting lines and numbers on several screens.

With the presence of the intricate systems and surgical equipment, the familiarity of the medical facility settled in.

But why was I here?

The thick mattress at my back kept me angled at forty-five degrees and allowed me to take in my setting while also giving false hope that I only had to take a step forward to freedom. That step was impossible.

Glancing down over my pale body, I tried to comprehend what prevented me from simply leaving. A panic surged through me when my eyes met the wide bands fastened across my hips and torso that held me in place.

"What's going on?" My voice came out groggy and weak. It was only then I craved liquid refreshment.

Neon green lines danced on the large monitor before me, and a robotic voice emitted from the machine's speaker. "Please stay calm. Your doctor has been notified of your restlessness and will be in to assist you shortly."

Instinct urged me to locate the door, which must've been out of my line of vision. And as I scanned the room, my impatience and panic transformed into full-on fear. I wanted out.

"Get me out of this thing!" I groaned and grunted against the unwanted embrace of the thick bands. The lines on the monitor displayed increasing peaks and valleys as I rocked and maneuvered. Its beeps rang in my ears before it instructed me to, "Please relax. Your doctor will be in shortly."

"Anyone?" I called out, ignoring the computer. "I want out. Get me out of here!"

I only paused when the click of the door opening and closing sounded from behind me. "Jovial?" A male voice questioned.

"Yes." He knew my name. Had the doctor finally arrived? "I want out of here."

The man appeared from behind with an unusual elegance, stepping before me like a performer stepping out from behind a curtain onto a stage. "It's good to see you all lively and such. How are you feeling? Do you know where you are?"

"Where's my mom?" was the only thing I needed to know. Something told me she would have all the answers.

"Your mother is here." He blinked slowly as he spoke, conveying a calm approach. "In fact, she is anxious to see you as soon as you are ready."

"I'm ready." I nodded before the words fully left my lips. "I want to see her now."

"Shortly." His smile sent a shudder down my spine as he pressed a small button on the frames of his glasses, activating a pinprick of light in the center of the frames, and shining it directly in my eyes as he visually examined them. "Do you know where you are?"

Again, with that question. I sneered, not willing to hide my unease. "I'm at a hospital." The more I thought about it the more confusing it became. "I am in a hospital, right? But why? What happened?"

"You have completed the lengthy process of your treatment." He angled his head to visually examine my nasal passages. "You look well, and your vitals are green, but how are you feeling?"

"I'm feeling..." I stared into his dark, round eyes and replayed his words in my head. "Treatment?"

By the way his nose twitched he wasn't satisfied with my answer. His cold fingers immediately went to my wrist, assessing. "Are you having difficulty remembering the program? It is normal if you are."

I searched my memory, seeing a small man sitting behind a large desk, pointing a bony finger my way. His scowl said more than his words. "I hereby order you, Jovial Spencer, to undergo a year of treatment in Deep Sleep."

"I remember." I nodded. A sense of elation briefly erased my unease as the memory came to me. Similar to getting the score of an exam to see I've miraculously aced it.

"What do you remember exactly?" He waited, observing me from the top of my dark curly hair to my French tip toes. His curiously unwrinkled and unsullied white lab coat stole my attention.

"Have I been under for an entire year?" I studied his inquisitive stare, anticipating his confirmation.

He nodded. "Indeed."

I imagined being asleep for twelve months and what changes may have occurred during that time, but the more I tried to focus on those things the more my curiosity dissipated. "It worked right?"

"That is left to be determined, but the surgery was successful." He went to one of the monitors and pressed on screen buttons. "Although there are several symptoms I hope to avoid. One being memory loss. However, a bit of memory issues this soon upon awakening is to be expected."

My nose tickled, yet I couldn't satisfy the itch with my arms confined at my sides. "Can I leave?"

"Let me be clear, you are not a prisoner." He continued to type and select info and notes through the system. "However, it is imperative that you are recovering as expected. So, please, try to be patient. Yes?"

The tickle in my nostrils grew more unbearable as seconds went by. I sniffed to alleviate the itch, but again the smokiness of charred peanut husks lingered. "What's that smell?"

"A smell, you say?" He finally turned and the pinprick of light emitted from the frame of his glasses, taking attention from his dark eyes. He was before me in seconds, breaching the invisible barriers of my personal space. "Open up, let me take a look."

Before I could fully comprehend his request, two fingers slipped past my lips and into my mouth. "Open wide," he ordered. I dry heaved when he used most of his fingers to pry my jaw open, then crooked his head and peered inside. I twisted and turned away, determined to distance myself from his probing. "Hold still now," he demanded, struggling to keep my head centered.

The scowl on his face mimicked the one from the judge in my memory, and although they were different people, their annoyance and impatience were similar.

Or was that a smile?

Instinctively, my tongue pushed at his ungloved fingers and the flavor of unwashed coins on my taste buds engaged my gag reflexes.

"Ah, I see." The pads of his fingers grazed the roof of my mouth. "The stitch in your palate has come undone."

He pressed the tissue and a bolt of pain shot through me as if that point was connected to every sensitive nerve webbed throughout my being. My entire body seized and remained rigid as I convulsed against the confines of the bed.

Screams of agony echoed throughout the room and blended with the beeps and sirens of the monitors.

Hot viscous liquid dripped down my chin and soaked the front of my gown with its warmth, and although my eyelids twitched involuntarily, glimpses of the doctor holding his wrist in one hand and shrieking in pain were communicated. Dark, contrasting red soiled his once pristine lab coat. It was then that the pain and fear surging through me was interrupted by a fleeting thought.

What a shame.

~~~

Thanks for reading. I enjoy feedback and would love to hear your thoughts!

2: Color Me Red

The color red swamped my vision, and enveloped me in an icky warmth as it dribbled from my lips and cast the room in its sickly hue.

"Are you feeling well, Jovial?"

I blinked and the bright lights overhead reflected off of the clean, white walls and it took a few seconds for my eyes to adjust, only to see the doctor standing before me in his immaculate white lab coat. Confused by his worried stare and unblemished clothing, I looked past him at the large machines and their systems projecting lines and numbers on several screens.

"What just happened?" My sights followed the seams of his coat down to his hands where his fingers were perfectly intact as if the entire bloody, panic-inducing incident never happened.

It happened. Didn't it?

He moved closer, aiming the light that shined from the center of his eyeglass frames in my face. "I examined the soft palate of your upper jaw to confirm the stitch is still there. In fact, it is. However, I suspect you may be experiencing some sort of cerebral trauma that is interfering with your ability to remember."

"What is cerebral trauma?" I narrowed my eyes, trying to read his facial expression while forcing myself to remain calm. "Brain damage?"

"Injury," he corrected. "Due to swelling at the surgical site. It can be repaired by healing, so I wouldn't categorize it as damage. As I mentioned before, with time it will heal, and your memory will gradually improve. In the meantime, your mother will assist you with your recollections."

Mom. Once again, I tested the bed's grip but the straps remained in place. "Where is she? I wanna see her."

"I will bring her in shortly." Instead, he returned to the monitors, using his fingers in perfect rhythm to type and click away at the onscreen buttons.

What had just happened? It couldn't have been my imagination. It felt so genuine. Every jolt of pain, the wailing of the alarms, the taste of his blood had seemed so real. Had it all been a result of a brain injury or had I somehow been dreaming?

I searched my memory for Mom, sensing that she would know how to fix the problem or at least ease me through the experience. Her short, slim frame, dark hair with tighter curls than mine, and unblemished dark brown skin popped into my mind. It was Dad and his features that eluded my memories. The only thing I could recall was his pale, untanned complexion and immense height.

What color were his eyes? His hair? The more I thought about those details the less I cared.

"I want my mom." I stared at the dark, wispy hairs mixed with gray at the back of the doctor's head. "I want to go home." Where was home and why I wanted to be there was uncertain. I felt it in my bones that home was where I needed to be.

The doctor pressed a button and a beep sounded from his monitor. "Send Ms. Spencer back to room two-thirty-seven, please."

There was no reply or confirmation. Only the occasional beeps and whirls of the machines penetrated the silence between us and the click of the door opening and closing behind me. "Mom?" My mouth craved liquids and moisture, but I ignored it for motherly assurance.

"Jo?" The warmth of her voice embraced me before she did. Appearing from my left, she first peaked around the edge of the bed before wrapping me in a one-sided hug. "Oh, look at you. Are you feeling okay? How's your memory?"

My memory? What about the fact that I am strapped to a bed and have been in Deep Sleep for a year? "I wanna go home."

"You will," she nodded, running her thumb across my cheek. "Oh, you will. I promise." She turned to the doctor. "How is she doing? Did the treatment work?"

"The treatment was successful." He bowed his head. "She is suffering from a few side effects, but as we discussed, she should be back to her old self in due time." He smiled and a sense of unease crept through me. What was it about his smile that put me off? Could it be that his smile mismatched what I was expecting, being that moments ago I had a mouthful of his blood dripping down my chin?

The thought of chomping down on his fingers made my stomach churn and a lump of queasiness lay at the base of my throat. The pit of my stomach quivered, and I forced myself to swallow the excess salvia pooling in my mouth. "Mom?"

"What about the side effects, Dr. Schwartz?" She went on, ignoring my call. "When my neighbor's son came out of Deep Sleep a couple months ago, he was discharged immediately with no symptoms. They haven't had any problems with him ever since." She snapped her head to look directly in my eyes. "Ian Rodgers? You remember Ian, don't you?"

Ian? Not even the name seemed familiar.

"That was a different case, Ms. Spencer." He clasped his hands together before him. "Every patient is different inside and out. And every patient requires individual correction, tailored specifically to their needs."

Was I supposed to know Ian? Why didn't his name spark a memory? "Did you do something to my brain?" I sneered, finally allowing the details to sink in. "Is that why there's swelling or injury?"

"This was discussed with you both before the procedure was done," he glanced to me. "You are having a difficult time remembering that." He cocked his head toward mother. "Ms. Spencer, you signed the contract detailing the risks and side effects and what your responsibilities would be when the patient awakens."

"I know." She huffed, barely letting him complete the sentence. "I'm just glad you're okay, Jo." She was at my side again, petting my hair like a beloved pet. "We have to celebrate, don't we? We have to do something special for your rebirthday."

My stomach fluttered and once again I swallowed down the sensation to vomit. I wanted water, food, and home. Celebrating was the last thing on my mind.

Mom tugged at the strap placed across my chest, holding me snug against the angled bed. "How much longer for this?"

"Until we are sure she will not unintentionally harm herself or others, it is only a precaution for her safety."

I was reluctant to reveal my nausea in fear that the doctor would want to keep me tied to the bed longer in order to run some tests or have me recover, but the fluttering in my stomach grew and the taste of bile at the back of my throat became more unpleasant. "Mom?"

She turned to me. "What's wrong?"

"I need water."

"Nothing in the mouth until the incision site is fully mended," the doctor butted in. "Your complaints about smelling smoke is quite concerning." His spine was strong and lengthened as he spoke. "But you are getting liquids and electrolytes through your IV."

Surprised that there was an IV, I finally recognized the line when I stared down at my wrists looking for it. "Oh." But an IV couldn't rinse the taste from my mouth.

"I'll leave you two to catch up for now." He glided across the room toward the exit.

As soon as the click of the door opening and closing sounded, and his footsteps were no longer audible near it, mom pressed her lips to my ear. "What do you remember?" Her hot breath made my earlobe moist as she spoke.

I shook my head. "Not much." Should I tell her about the bloody incident that I experienced earlier, or would that urge her to keep me here longer?

"You don't remember anything at all?" She searched my face with wide eyes and for the first time I sensed her fear.

"Mom, what's going on?" I felt the hot sting of tears well up in my eyes. "I'm scared and just want to go home."

"I want you to come home too, Jo," she whispered, aggressively and absentmindedly rubbing the back of my hand. "If he believes everything is going as planned, he will let you come home."

"What do you mean?" I shook my head in confusion, taking in a whiff of stringent alcohol on her breath. "What's wrong with me?"

"Nothing's wrong except the stuff with your memory. That was the one side effect or risk we were afraid of." Deep wrinkles appeared at the center of her forehead.

She had nothing to worry about. "He said it will come back to me though."

"It will, but he needs to believe it already has." She wanted me to do something. Something I wouldn't be able to understand unless she told me, and judging by her behavior, speaking it aloud was the difficult part.

I stared at her in silence while she nodded, encouraging my participation. I gulped. "So, what do I do?"

"Tell him you remember Ian Rodgers, that you were in love and that you want to see him. That you miss him." She rubbed my shoulder reassuringly. "Can you do that, honey? Don't you want to come home?"

Ian Rodgers? "But—"

Before I could answer, a wave of nausea hit me. I tried to close my lips, but a stream of red tinged liquid spewed from my mouth and into her face. She didn't scream as I expected her to, instead she rushed around the room to collect clothes and clean it up in silence. After quickly wiping her face of the residue, she used a fresh cloth to dab at mine, repeating, "It's okay. You're fine. You're just fine."

3: Inside

The tinge of red settled and dried in the crevices of Mom's broad nose and around her eyelids. Looking at her reminded me of my own features, and it was then that I realized we shared similar traits.

I remembered others comparing our physical appearance, and me taking pride in what she passed down to me. However, pain wouldn't allow me to reminisce too long.

A quiver in the pit of my stomach took me out of my thoughts as Mom wiped my lips like an infant after a filling meal. Except my stomach was empty of food or water and still fluttered and ached. Instinct told me to take the cloth from her and clean myself, but the straps held me snug in place.

"You'll be okay, Jo," she reassured, wiping my neck with a moist end of the cloth. Footsteps approached in the hall and she paused, frozen with a look of astonishment. Probably debating what to do next. "I need to get rid of these." She frantically rushed around the room, barely avoiding collision with the monitors and bulky equipment as she whipped back and forth to clean up the last traces of vomit.

She dropped the cloths in the trash bin just as the room door clicked and the tap of meticulous footsteps grew louder as they got closer.

She stood in front of me, scanning the room with worry in her eyes, not realizing the traces of evidence painted in the crooks of her face and clothes.

As Dr. Schwartz turned the corner he gasped. "Ms. Spencer? What on earth happened to you?"

She sighed in defeat. "It was an accident, but everything's alright. She'll be just fine."

He turned to me with wide eyes, switching on his flashlight. "Open. Let me take a look."

The thought of allowing him entry into my mouth, even to observe, made me grimace. Shaking my head in defiance, I made my refusal clear. "No."

"This may very well be a life-threatening situation." He glared, his dark eyes indicating his frustration. "Now, open up."

"No!" I turned my head away and clenched my teeth together, preparing for a repeat of my memory. He would have to pry my jaw open with a crowbar if he wanted to see inside.

He shook his head in annoyance, still holding back his anger that I sensed bubbled under the surface. "Ms. Spencer, excuse us please."

"You want me to leave?" She shook her head just as I did. "I want to stay. I want to know what's going on."

He rushed to the monitors, pressed a few buttons, and then the loud beeps and alarms began to reverberate inside the room. "I will have to sedate her to examine her wound thoroughly. It is a delicate process and only staff is allowed during that process. So please, Ms. Spencer. Your cooperation is imperative."

I shook my head to object, but it took much more effort to control my muscles than anticipated. Had he already given me the sedative? "Mom?" I managed, but my lips were not moving as quickly as I wanted. "Don't—" The words played out in my head but wouldn't escape my mouth. If I did what she had told me to, would he stop? Would he listen? "Ian," I whispered, trying to muster up the strength to fight the hands of sleep that threatened to pull me under. "Ian Rodgers."

Relief overwhelmed me as I gave in and allowed my muscles to relax and my eyes to close.

I blinked against the stark white of the room. Grogginess threatened to yank me back to sleep, but I fought it, tensing my muscles to bring them back to life.

"Jo?" Mom's soothing voice was in my ear. "Wake up, Jo."

I blinked again, trying desperately to have my body match my intentions. "Mom?"

"Yes, I'm here." Her smile was evident in her tone. "You did good, honey. You did so good."

My eyes met hers and my head slumped forward. Was she sitting in a chair? Was I? I glanced at my wrists which were bound to the armrests of a metal chair with a leather strap. I yanked, testing its strength.

"Don't hurt yourself now." She patted the back of my hand to stop me. "That's only there for your safety. Okay? You'll be out of that soon."

"What happened?" I managed to lift my heavy head and look into her worried eyes.

"What do you remember?"

Not this. Not now. "Please, Mom. I don't want to talk about memories." I took in a deep breath to fully awaken, no longer smelling burnt anything.

"It's important, Jo." She rubbed my shoulder to comfort me. "If you want to come home we have to go through the process. So, what do you remember?"

The process. So, there were rules and I had to play by them. "Blood." I smacked my lips together, trying to clear the rusty taste from my mouth. "I remember him putting his disgusting fingers in my mouth and biting him. His blood was everywhere." When I met her gaze again, the motherly worry I was used to seeing turned into uncertainty.

"But—" Her head teetered back and forth in her shoulders. "You didn't bite anyone."

"Was I dreaming?" A dream that vivid would convince anyone it was real.

She nodded uncomfortably slow. "It sounds like you were. Do you remember anything else?"

"You." I examined the crevices around her nose and eyes, and although there was no longer any trace of red, I was hesitant to ask if that was just a nightmare too. "Vomit?"

"Yes." She moved closer, sitting on the edge of her chair. "They examined you while you were under and, good news, you're fine! There are no ulcers or open wounds. The doctor thinks the incision in the roof of your mouth could have been bleeding and you may have swallowed some of the blood, but you're okay."

Could that explain the uncomfortable sensation in my gut? "Good."

"What about before?" She narrowed her eyes and leaned closer. "Do you remember anything?"

I lifted an eyebrow, testing. "Ian Rogers?"

Her eyes lit up. "So, you remember him?"

"Only the name." I shrugged. "Who is he?"

A wave of disappointment erased her brief enthusiasm. "He's the neighbor's son. He went through Deep Sleep treatment over a year ago and they brought him back home a couple months ago."

"Was he ordered to do treatment like me?"

"Of course, he was ordered. Not many kids have a choice, you know." She finally sat back, relaxing a bit. "It seems like only the wealthy take liberty in using this place like a babysitting service. Your kid won't clean their room? Send them to Deep Sleep. Need a break from your unruly teens? Send them to Deep Sleep. Want a vacation from being a parent? Send your kids to Deep Sleep. It should be illegal, I swear. Every year they come out with some new thing everyone wants to try or take advantage of."

Irritation screamed from her dismissive hand waves and eye rolls. "What do you mean?"

She swiped the air. "Nothing, I'm just complaining." She huffed and sat forward again. "Ian Rodgers was ordered to Deep Sleep for theft. He stole over ten thousand dollars' worth of stuff in a year. All kinds of stuff, jewelry, clothes, food. Since he awakened a couple of months ago, he's been the sweetest kid. Fully rehabilitated. Never stole a thing since or even get the urge to swipe something."

I tried to put it all together but was still confused. "What does he have to do with me?"

"He was your boyfriend. Or at least it was thought he was. You never told me about him, but then again you never really told me anything. You mentioned him in your diary though." She dropped her gaze in an attempt to hide her shame.

"Why am I here?"

"It's—" she huffed, hesitating. "It's complicated."

"Complicated?" Didn't I have a right to know why I was ordered to Deep Sleep? "They did something to my brain while I was sleeping, and I want to know what and why."

"I don't want to upset you." Her hands trembled and she clasped them together in her lap to prevent it. "You've been through a lot."

I yanked the straps with my wrists and tried to stand, realizing my ankles were secured to the legs of the chair. "Tell me." I growled, ignoring the pain. "Tell me now. Why am I here?"

With fear in her eyes, she stuttered until her response was clear. "Some of the stuff he stole was in your possession. You were an accomplice."

I gave in to the pain around my wrists and relaxed in my seat. "Why? Why would we steal these things? For money?"

"Yeah, maybe." She shrugged, and for a moment I wondered if I looked like her whenever I shrugged. "No one really knows. Neither of you ever confessed or denied anything. You both always stayed quiet, but the evidence spoke for you."

I checked my memory for a reason. Only seeing a brief glimpse of my mouth romantically on another's. Had Ian and I been a couple? How close were we and why would we do the things we were accused of? "I'm confused."

"It's okay." She patted my hand. "It will all come back to you."

The urge to rub my temples to encourage my memory was interrupted by the realization that I was bound to a chair. "I want to leave." Anger quickly bubbled to the surface. "I want out of this place. Why won't they let me leave?"

"Safety reasons." Her voice was gentle.

I wasn't convinced. "Bullshit."

"Jo?" She seemed shocked at my behavior. "This isn't you and acting like this will get us nowhere."

If this wasn't me then who was I? I blinked, trying to remember my personality, my goals, my desires. Frustration was the only thing I connected with. Why couldn't I remember who I was? "What did he do to me? What did he do to my brain?"

"It's okay, Jo." Mom's gentle voice had no effect. "He treated the problem. That's what he does. He just has to see that your memory is undamaged."

My stomach churned again, and I desperately wanted to clench my gut to ease the pain but couldn't. Instead I belted over in my seat. "I hate this. I want it to stop." I dry heaved as the rancid taste returned to my taste buds overpowering my senses. "Why is this happening?"

"What's happening?" Mom stood, rubbing my shoulder to little relief. "Tell me what's wrong."

"I'm woozy. My stomach hurts." Wave after wave of nausea hit me and I didn't want to move until it subsided. Then the flutter became all too real as it moved from one side of my stomach to the other. I gasped. Wide eyes locked onto hers. "Oh, my god."

"What's wrong?" She knelt before me, urging me to speak. "You gotta tell me what's wrong so I can fix it."

My fists tightened into balls as I mimicked herworried stare. "There's something inside of me."

~~~

Any thoughts? Share them below.

4: Hands Off

The inside of my belly fluttered again and the thought of something living inside of my body made me scream. "There's something in there! Something's inside of me." I thrashed my upper body back and forth in the chair, yanking at the straps around my wrists and ankles.

"Jo, wait." Mom's hands went to my shoulders to keep me still. "Hold on. Calm down."

Beeping, footsteps, and audible whirls of machines were prematurely drowned out by my cries. "I want out. Let me out."

Dr. Schwartz appeared as if summoned by the computer's alarms. "She's experiencing a mental breakdown. We have to put her under."

"No," I protested. "No more sleep." I just wanted the nightmare to end. "No more blood. No more sleep. I want to go home. Just let me go home." My sobs did little to comfort me and my pleas did nothing to stop the darkness from slowly seeping in and taking over.

My muscles relaxed like noodles and I lay in a pool of blackness. Steady rhythmic beeps and alarms surrounded me until the familiar sound of Dr. Schwartz's voice crept in.

"We performed this procedure thousands of times on various patients and had been successful but for a small percentage. Ms. Spencer, I am afraid Jovial is one of those unfortunate cases."

"Just let me work with her, Doctor." Mom's voice lifted my spirits. "Just give me time with her, and I promise she will turn out to be one of your greatest success stories." Her voice quivered and it was then that I recognized the hint of uncertainty.

Fleeting moments of stark white and mother's worried eyes went by. Interesting sounds faded in and out and time was no longer relevant.

It was only until I opened my eyes again, that I realized I had been asleep. "Mom?" She slouched in a chair across from my bed. With her eyes closed and her torso draped over the armrest, her breathing deepened. Was she asleep? "Mom?"

Her head rose and her sights landed on me. "Jo!" Enthusiasm lit up her face. She rushed to my side as I lay flat and still against the hospital bed mattress. Grogginess and the bright lights blurred my vision and instinct urged me to block the light with my hand.

My palm hovered over my eyes and I smiled when I was able to see her face more clearly. My heart filled with warmth knowing I didn't wake up alone and that she sacrificed a comfy bed and decent sleep to be here when I awoke.

After a few seconds, the realization that my arms were no longer bound hit me. I sat up, taking no time to lift my shirt and examine my stomach.

"It's okay, honey." Mom ran her delicate fingers through the tangles of my hair. "You've been through a lot. I know, but don't worry."

I pressed on my abdominal muscles with my fingers to provoke the strange and uncomfortable flutter, but instead seen and felt nothing out of the ordinary, only my flat unblemished belly. "It felt like something was moving around in there. I could've sworn something was inside of me." When I caught a glimpse of her expression, I added, "And I know I wasn't dreaming when I felt it."

"I know. I know," she whispered in her gentle and soothing voice. "The doctor explained how that happens when your stomach hasn't had to digest food or water for a while. It's uncomfortable but normal." She continued to play with my matted strands. "I just don't want you to worry. You've been through a lot and worrying will only add to the stress."

I didn't want to worry either, but what other reaction would be appropriate in this predicament? How was I supposed to absorb what was happening to me while experiencing such prolonged fear? "How long have I been asleep?"

Her fingers stopped combing and she paused. "You just completed your year in treatment."

I huffed, a sense of frustration building in me. Did she really think my memory was that damaged? "I don't mean since waking from Deep Sleep. I mean, how long did he have me sedated?"

"Oh, um." She continued raking her fingers through my curls. "It's been almost a couple days."

"Days?" I shook my head, trying to understand while searching for signs of the passing days in her change of clothes. "Why was I asleep for so long?"

She sighed. Tucking a ringlet of my hair behind my ear. "There are ... complications."

"Oh no." I crooked my neck to judge the seriousness in her facial expressions.

"Listen." Her eyes widened as she grabbed my forearms in her firm grip. "I don't want you freak out, okay? You got to try and stay calm and be reasonable." Something about her grasp didn't sit well with me and I refused to remove my gaze from her hands. "There are some complications he's trying to figure out how to fix. Something went wrong and the problem is not only with your memory, but your personality, your behaviors. It's not like you."

I pulled away from her grip with a forceful twist of my wrist. "Keep your hands off of me." I glared, finally removing my focus from my arms to meet her stare.

Her jaw dropped and she backed away. It was only then that I spotted the two-tier white cake with red letter frosting on the table behind her. My legs were heavy as I swung them over the edge of the mattress to get a better look at the treat. Weaving between the many candles, the red letters spelled out: Happy Rebirthday, Jo.

Instinctively, I sniffed the air to take in the sweet scent of frosting, only getting a trace of smoke instead. With the faint stench of char hovering in my sinuses, it reminded me that I wasn't allowed to eat or drink until my palate was fully healed. Besides, the cake looked unappetizing anyway.

The room door and going through it was the only thing I craved.

When I put pressure on my legs to stand, they wobbled, and I immediately crashed back onto the bed.

"Careful." With a bit of hesitation, Mom came to my assistance, hoisting me back up on the mattress more securely.

"What's wrong with me?" I flexed my legs and wiggled my toes. "Why can't I walk?

"You've been in treatment for a while, Jo." Her tone was dry and matter of fact. "This is what happens when you haven't walked or used your muscles for some time. It's normal."

"But I was fine before." I shook my head, not convinced by her explanation. "Sitting in the chair, I remember using my leg muscles to try to stand but I was strapped down."

"Oh, Jo. I'm so worried about you." Sadness flooded her eyes in the form of tears. "You're scaring me. Everything. All of this. It's scaring me." Her hand trembled as she brought it to her lips to ineffectively hold back her sobs.

A similar memory flooded my mind like a case of déjà vu. Mom in tears, sitting on the floor in front of a half-emptied wine bottle. Her slurred ramblings about hating who she was and the way her life turned out, and how she was forced to give up her childhood to "do it" alone.

Before I could delve deeper into the recollection another forced its way to the forefront. An attractive young man with dark brown hair and eyes. Although his ethnic facial features reminded me of my own, his unblemished darker skin tone drew me in. His smile caused my heart to triple in beat and the urge to see him came on strong. Was that Ian?

Another glimpse flooded my memories of agile fingers on the keys of a piano and the melodic sound of my voice filling the air. What was happening? I needed answers but those answers didn't reside in this room or in this hospital. "I'm ready to go home."

"And I want you to come home, baby. I do."

"But?" I sneered, knowing the answer before she had a chance to give me her somber puppy eyes.

She sighed, passing time or possibly trying to find the best way to let me down easy. "I told you, there were complications the doctor needs to treat before he discharges you."

"So, you're gonna allow him to keep me here against my will?" Anger rose as heat to my chest and I allowed it to sweep aside any sense of reason.

"Jo, remember," she gestured with her hands, signaling me to be aware of my reaction, "you have to calm down."

Fear and uncontrollable irritation at realizing my vulnerability built up. Did I have no say in the matter at all? "He can't keep me like this, Mom?"

"For your wellbeing he can." She nodded, only fueling my anger. "And as much as I don't like it, it's what's best for you. You're sick, honey. You have to be healed. It's his duty to have you go home treated and it's his right to do what is necessary to make that happen."

"His right?" I clenched the bedsheet in my fists. "What about my rights?"

"I know. I know. I don't like it either, but the only choice we have is to play by the rules." She pleaded with her eyes. "Do you understand?"

I shook my head, not willing to be further subjected to his torture. Using all my arm strength I pushed myself up to stand. Against Mom's protests I balanced and took a step, immediately collapsing to the floor. When she tried to come to my aid again, I pushed her away. "No. leave me alone," I snarled. If she was willing to have me lay around in this hospital and rot until I was treated, how much assistance could she be anyway?

I ignored her pleas and used my arms to drag myself across the cold tiles to the door. I reached out to hook my fingers around the door handle that didn't turn. It was no surprise that I was locked in. What did surprise me was Mom standing before the cake with tears in her eyes, pretending to light the candles, and declaring, "Come on, Jo. Let's celebrate."

~~~

As always, your feedback is appreciated.

5: Paint Me Void

Although the candles in the cake were not alive with flame, I could easily imagine the smoke it would have produced as my imagination blended in with my recent memory of burnt almonds.

With my back against the cold steel door of the private hospital room, the cogs were turning in my head trying to understand what Mom was doing as her shaky voice rose in an off tuned and altered rendition of Happy Birthday. "Happy Rebirthday to you." She waved her hand, gesturing, urging me to go over and pretend to blow out the candles.

I stared, baffled, waiting for her to acknowledge my lack of interest, my weak legs, and their inability to carry my weight. Did she really want me to use my arms to drag my body across the cold, dirty floor to indulge in make-believe?

"I just want to bring some normalcy back into our lives." She pleaded with her eyes. "So, come on, honey. Make a wish."

Her desperation and drive were obvious. I questioned rather I should continue to be reluctant or play along. Ever since waking from

Deep Sleep, she's been asking me to play by the rules. Doing so could be key to getting out of this place. But who's rules? The doctor's? The system's? Society's? Maybe she knew something about the rules I didn't.

"I wish," I started, thinking long and hard for the exact words that would resonate. "I wish everything was back to normal." As soon as the words left my lips, a river of tears ran down her cheeks and for a while her sniffles were the only sound in the room.

"Oh, how I wish we didn't have to go through this. Things were bad enough before, but I thought I could fix it. I just didn't work hard enough and it's all my fault." Her shoulders slumped forward and she covered her face with both hands as she sobbed. "I don't know what changed. Just one day it all became really hard."

"What did?" My voice cracked and I gulped down any trace of pity.

"Raising you." She sniffed, wiping away the moisture that collected below her nose with the back of her hand. "Not many people know how hard it is to raise a young woman and do it alone. Maybe that's why this program came into being. Who knows?" She shrugged and continued to wipe away tears before they reached her discolored cheeks. "I think you hated me. That's why it was so stressful."

I cocked my head, trying hard to access my sealed memory bank. "I hated you? Why?"

"No, you didn't hate me, just the person I became when alcohol got into me. It was as if you'd looked at me and see the future you. It probably scared and angered you, understandably. And your resentment wasn't easy to hide. You wanted better from me and I let you down."

"Oh." For the first time, I found it hard to meet her gaze. As a pang of guilt echoed in my chest. Was my resentment toward her what brought me here? Had I been acting out in defiance because of her alcohol dependency?

"But I didn't blame you," she went on. "You had it all. Your talents and abilities always impressed me. You had so much to offer and there I was mucking it up."

The memory of black and white ivory keys entered my mind. "Piano?"

"Yes!" Her eyes widened. "Exactly. You remember? And singing. You sang so beautifully. Sometimes I wished I had your voice and your talent. Well, not sometimes but all the time." She chuckled. "You must've gotten it from your daddy, because I'm just a useless, empty husk with nothing to offer." She tried to laugh at her joke, but the laugher came out lackluster. "You had everything anyone could wish for. You were filled with so much creative potential."

If I had it all, how did I end up here enclosed in sanitary surroundings with little awareness of who I was or the crimes I had committed? "Then what happened?"

She shook her head, staring at the white and red frosted cake. "I don't know."

Neither did I and I wondered if I ever would. Searching my memory didn't produce answers, only a headache and more confusion.

There had to be more to understand what would cause me to break the law. There had to be more answers at home. "When can we leave?"

"When the doctor says you're ready."

From the way it's been going, things seemed to get worse than better. "What if he never says I'm ready, will I be stuck here forever?" Was that even a possibility?

"No, I won't let that happen." But she avoided looking my way when she said it, choosing to stare down the cake instead.

"What's wrong?" I urged, reading her body language. "You're not telling me something."

She sighed. "I don't want you to be upset."

I sat forward, pulling away from the door at my back while taking note that the nerves in my feet were slowly waking. "If you keep things from me, how can we form any semblance of trust?" I was careful not to raise my voice or show any form of hostility. "You're my mom, and I want to believe you have my best interest at heart."

She finally turned to me. "Look at you, sounding so mature." Pointing it out gave me pause as I wondered if maturity was initially part of my personality. She continued, "I want you to come home as much as you want to, but I'm afraid that something will go wrong and then they'll be forced to keep you here. That's why it's important you cooperate. Keep things running smoothly."

"What do you mean, keep me here?" My eyebrows pulled together as I tried reading between the lines. "You mean keep me in this place forever?"

"There's been rumors, okay." She lowered her voice to an unnerving whisper. "I don't know who started them, so I don't want to spread them and make you worry."

"Oh, you have to tell me now," I demanded, throwing all caution to the wind.

"Jo, I want you to get better—"

I put my hand up, dismissing her excuses. "Trust, remember?"

She glanced behind her at the chair she had awakened on and forgone its comfort to sit on the cold tiles before me. "Rumors been circulating about Deep Sleep and the facility. One rumor in particular says a girl has been in the facility for six years, ever since she was twelve years old. The rumor goes, this girl claims the doctors were experimenting with space and time by placing her soul or consciousness into different dimensions."

I narrowed my eyes. "Is that even possible?"

"Deep Sleep rehabilitation has been in operation for merely a decade, the technology is still considered new and ever evolving, that's why so many rumors are out there. A lot of people don't understand the process or know exactly how the treatment is done, so they make up their own myths and stories. This is only a rumor."

"One you believe." We locked eyes and an ominous chill crept over me. It made sense. She's been urging me to play nice, so I won't get trapped here and experimented on. "Every year they come up with a new thing someone wants to try or take advantage of. You said so yourself."

"That's just my nerves talking." She swiped the air dismissively. "But..." She gave me a serious look. "Just in case it isn't, we have to try to make your rehabilitation work. You will be one of his biggest success stories, just you watch. You'll be the next media sensation and no one would dream of making you stay here longer than necessary. I promise. We gotta work on getting your memory back and showing that you've been rehabilitated and then he'd be convinced to send you home."

So, she did believe the rumors. How much of it could be true? Removing and transferring human consciousnesses and messing around with space, time, and other dimensions seemed like a plot straight out of a science fiction movie. But we were at a point in technology where a person could be put to sleep for an entire year and wake up fully reformed. Was transferring human consciousnesses really that impossible?

In fact, just how much was done or manipulated with me or my brain while I was under? How long have I been here, only one year or six like the rumored girl? Come to think of it, did I actually wake up at all or did they successfully transfer my consciousness to another dimension and my body is still asleep in reality.

I gulped at the memory of Dr. Schwartz's fingers and blood in my mouth, and immediately my mind grasped fractions of a famous Plato quote, "How can you prove whether ... we are sleeping, or whether we are awake, and talking ... in the waking state?" Although I had difficulty remembering the quote fully, I knew somehow those words were important.

And the more I tried to analyze what was real or a dream, the more confused I became. I didn't feel like myself even though I had no idea what being myself felt like. Everything seemed wrong, or skewed, and unrealistic? Was what I was experiencing part of a different reality or part of a dream world? Was the reason I couldn't support my body weight was because in reality I was asleep? Much like not being able to run from danger in a dream only to wake and realize the bedsheets were tangled around my legs, making me believe I were incapable?

My thoughts would have forever wandered if it wasn't for the return of the coiling in my gut, my intestines twisted, and a sharp pain caught me off guard.

"No. Not again." I doubled over in pain, grunting and grimacing to keep myself from screaming and conjuring Dr. Schwartz. When will this nightmare be over? When will I wake up?

"Come on," Mom urged as she stood. "Let's get you back in bed." She gently eased me to the bed and we both struggled to get me under the sheet and reclined against the firm pillows.

The twisting slowly subsided, but my breathing hastened as beads of sweat dampened my forehead. "What's happening to me, Mom?" Something told me she would know.

She shook her head and tried to instill a sense of comfort in me by rubbing my shoulder. "Your body is trying to heal. It's not easy but it'll get there."

"Do you think they did something to me that they weren't supposed to do while I was sleeping?" I stared at her, waiting for her admission. "Be honest with me." I searched her face for the words she refused to speak, and wondered why she wouldn't make eye contact. "I want to trust you, Mom. I really do."

"You don't?" She finally connected with me, seeming offended by my words. "I'm being open and honest."

"Was something done to my mind and body that I wasn't aware of?" I waited, wanting to hear the words from her lips.

"Absolutely not." She didn't even flinch.

My mind raced with billions of possibilities and scenarios, but one in particular stood out from the rest. "Was I experimented on like the rumors say? Tell me the truth."

"No, I would never allow that." Her face twisted in anger. "I would never consent to anything like that. And if I found out something unlawful happened to you without my knowledge I would riot in the streets. I love you too much, Jo."

As I wiggled and flexed my toes under the sheet, testing their strength, I placed my palm over the slight flutter in my gut, preparing to do what I had to do to find the truth and go home. Maybe home had the answers. Not what was at home but who. Ian Rogers.

~~~

What do you think is happening? Any theories?

6: Release Me

According to my memory, Ian possessed a strong jawline for a nineteen-year-old. His dark facial hair speckled his chin, and his deep brown eyes reminded me of my own. His prominent African American features dominated his physical appearance with a broad nose and thicker lips.

Ian Rodgers had to be the significant link between my lost memories and answers. A lot of who I was seemed to be connected to him.

"I want to see Ian." After mom looked at me funny, I added, "Maybe seeing him will help trigger some memories. And that's what we want, right? For me to remember?"

She nodded, but I can tell by the look on her face that she was against the idea. "I want you to get back home so you can see him too, but Dr. Schwartz refuses to discharge you until you're better."

"Why not bring him to me?" My eyes grew wide with the idea and I nodded to encourage her to agree. She took a while contemplating, so I added, "Having him visit would be a really nice rebirthday gift."

Just the thought of him took my mind off of the horrific experiences I've been through since waking from treatment, but it only fueled more questions. Did he miss me and was patiently waiting for my return? Had he questioned if I were okay or not, was he looking for answers as well?

"I'll see what I can do." She huffed and glided her hands over the sheet of my bed while staring longingly at the white and red cake. I stared too, wondering if she was willing to eat it alone. "Sorry." She frowned. "Doctor says no food or drink yet."

"I know." I nodded, trying to remain cooperative and pleasant. "I'm not really hungry." And the charred smell that lingered in the back of my throat made it difficult to conjure up an appetite anyway.

"Are you still in pain?" She came to my side, her brown eyes drooped in sympathy.

"No, I feel better." I confessed, trying to pinpoint the exact location of the previous flutter.

"Do you remember anything other than the piano? Has any more memories returned to you?"

I bobbed my head. "I think I remember Ian." Her eyes widened, causing a bit of eagerness to rush through me. "He has a darker skin tone than me, right? Short tight curls on his head. Stocky, athletic body?"

"That's right!" She pressed her hands together excitedly, as if she wanted to clap but stopped herself from going full in.

"How was he as a person?" I wished I could remember more than his physical appearance. I couldn't even recall the sound of his voice or any of his quirks or mannerisms.

"He used to play football in high school. After he graduated, things changed. Everything changed, really. He kind of lost interest in football."

"Really? Why?"

She shrugged and frowned, causing a crinkle in her forehead. "I don't know much. I only know what I've learned after you were sent here."

I stared out the corner of my eye, waiting for her to explain. "What else do you know about him?"

"He's a handsome young man. I'm sure he attracted a lot of eyes, but he didn't seem interested in any other girl but you." She smiled but it was off and appeared forced.

I cocked my head. "He told you that?"

"Well, not exactly." Her shoulders tensed as she lifted them. "The only thing that matters is that he would love to see you go home."

"But how are you so sure?" I wasn't satisfied with her explanations. I wanted to remind her of trust but repeating the word would be futile. Either way, bringing up trust would only give away that I lacked it. "Have you talked to him since he returned from Deep Sleep? Does he remember me? Does he ask about me?"

"I didn't get a chance to talk to him yet, but—"

"I don't understand." I shook my head, trying to read between the lines at what she wasn't saying. "Talk to me, please. I'm already so confused I need you to help me piece things together."

"There are ways to help you recollect your memories and telling you everything isn't the way to do it. I want you to pull up that information yourself and not have it fed to you." She rubbed the sheet again, this time over my feet. "I can give you bits but not everything."

Then why had she mentioned Ian in the first place and encourage me to convince Dr. Schwartz that I had remembered him? I narrowed my eyes suspiciously. "I want to see him. Seeing him might trigger something and help me remember."

She nodded but didn't move, giving the cake a melancholy stare.

A ball of anger bubbled up in my chest and strained my ribcage as I tried desperately to hold it in and not allow it to erupt. "So, when can I see him? When will you tell him I'm okay and waiting to return to him?"

"I'll have to talk to Dr. Schwartz about it first."

"Why do you have to tell him anything?" I didn't trust him at all, something about the way he operated unnerved me. Not to mention that horrific dream of chomping down on his disgusting fingers. I shuddered at the memory. It only sparked suspicion as to what vile and unfortunate acts took place for the year I was in Deep Sleep. "What if the rumors are true and Dr. Schwartz is experimenting on his patients? On me?"

"Then we'll do what we need to do to put a stop to it and make it right." She didn't sound convincing in the slightest, and the way she spoke made me question how much influence she had. Did she have the power to stop him or was she putting on a facade to satisfy me? I wasn't convinced that she could prevent anything from taking place, especially since she didn't even have the authority to get me home.

"Isn't there a saying that some parts of a rumor are true?"

"This is why I didn't want to bring up those rumors, Jo. You're going to stress out over it and frankly we have no proof or even a reason to question Dr. Schwartz at this stage."

I narrowed my eyes. "Don't you want me out of here?"

"I do."

"So why talk to him about Ian?"

"Didn't I say we have to play the game?" Her voice came out in a whisper. "This is part of it. We have to follow the rules. We can't go making our own. Maybe I can convince him to discharge you, but it will require your cooperation." Her voice was so low, I watched her lips to read them. "Give him what he needs, and he should be willing to give us what we need." Before I could protest, she continued, "That means allowing him to examine you and make sure you're okay inside and out and maybe he'd be more generous with your privileges."

I sat back against the cold pillows, feeling defeated. I had no say over where my life was headed, and the realization only frustrated me. The only thing running through my mind was the need to get out of this disgustingly sterile room. I allowed the pillows to cradle my form and the rhythmic beeping of machines to lull me to a relaxed state.

If enough time went by, maybe I could feign sleep and she would get tired, bored, or stir crazy enough to leave the room and allow me to get a better glimpse of an escape. I closed my eyes and let my breathing dive deep but remain steady as I counted the passing minutes in my head.

"Jo?" Her soft voice nearly caused me to open my eyes in response, but when I didn't, she moved to the nearest computer that continually beeped despite having no direct line to gather my vitals. The sound of her fingernails tapping on the screen prompted me to open my eyes a sliver to witness her actions.

With her back to me, her body blocked the monitor. Curiosity urged me to watch and try to decipher her actions, but she pivoted, and I closed my eyes again. The clink of the door lock disengaging startled me. Thankfully, I suppressed a jolt and successfully hid all signs that I was awake as her footsteps pitter-pattered toward the door. Nonetheless, the realization hit me. She had access to the lock this entire time.

I debated if I should take a chance and make a run for it as soon as the door opened or wait until I was better prepared and informed about what lay beyond the threshold. What awaited me out there? More locked doors? Dr. Schwartz himself? His aides? If so, would trying to leave now ruin my chance to escape?

The door opened and the chill of outside air crept into the room as if it was an entity itself. I shuddered but continued to pretend to be asleep as her footsteps disappeared into the hall. The door closed behind her, engaging the lock with another loud click.

I sat up and immediately threw the sheet aside and my legs over the edge of the bed to stand. Finally, I was able to support my weight but not without effort. My knees buckled but I managed to stay balanced. Carefully, I teetered on one foot then the other, making my way to the computer ahead of me.

Its bulk took up a significant amount of space in the room and its beeps grew louder but remained steady as I approached. For a brief second, the rhythmic pulse in the form of lines on the screen mesmerized me as I stared, questioning what information it was keeping track of and how.

There were no tubes connected to me like the one in my wrist when I first awakened. And upon further examination, there wasn't even a cord attached to connect it to an electrical source, but it continued to function with its constant noise and dancing lines.

I tapped the screen, trying to replicate what I saw Dr. Schwartz do many times. There was no response. Nothing on the screen changed. What did Mom do to activate it and unlock the door? My fingers pressed different parts of the screen, when a computerized voice screeched through the machine's speakers. "Please stay calm. Your doctor has been notified of your restlessness and will be in to assist you shortly."

"No." My heart raced at the thought of being sedated or restricted to my bed or a chair again, and the monitor reflected my panic with its increasingly high pitch beeps. "No, wait. I don't need the doctor."

"Please stay calm and back away from the equipment." The voice warned, but I ignored it, tapping on the screen more quickly and aggressively. "Please refrain from touching the equipment."

"Open the door," I demanded and anchored myself by holding onto the monitor with one hand while beating the console with the other.

"Step away from the equipment." Loud sirens screeched around me, causing me to block the noise by placing my palms over my ears. I could barely maintain my balance and nearly collapsed to the hard tile. But I watched in horror as the machine unfolded and expanded with a well-lubricated mechanism of smooth and shiny metal gliding silently over each other to produce two slender contraptions that resembled arms with claw-like fingers attached to the ends of each.

With sophisticated twists, spins, twirls, and coils, the individual rods extended and clamped its cold metal around my wrist. I yanked and pulled but was no match as the machine refused to budge.

"Let me go!" I fought, thrashing my body around in the effort to off center it or break its clutch. When that proved fruitless, I gripped its arm with my free hand. When it squeezed tighter, I screamed in agony, anticipating the imminent crunch of bone beneath its grip.

"Your doctor will be in shortly."

~~~

Your feedback is valuable! Please share your thoughts and feel free to point out any errors or inconsistencies. It's all appreciated. Thanks.

7: Open Book

I snapped my eyes open and sat upright in bed, blinded by the stark white. "What's going on?"

Mom twisted her face in worry as she rushed to my side. "You've had an episode and passed out in bed. How do you feel?"

I glared, not hesitating to show my doubt. "Don't tell me that was a dream." I shot my sights to the monitor, which continued its rhythmic beeps and projecting its glowing green lines on the screen. "That thing grabbed me. I know it did." I could still feel the remnants of its cold, steel fingers around my wrists and lifted them, expecting to showcase a bruise but only seeing even lightly bronzed skin tone stare back at me.

She patted my head. "Relax, Jo—"

"Stop telling me to relax." I jerked away from her comforting palm. My glare was vicious, I felt the tension in every muscle. "Where did you go, huh? How did you get out of here?"

She nodded; a streak of guilt flashed across her face. "While you were sleeping, I went to talk to Ian to convince him to come and see you."

"And?" I twisted in bed to stare at the door, anticipating someone standing there.

"And ..." She shook her head, sadness and defeat made up her facial features. "I'm sorry."

I tossed the sheet aside and threw my legs over the edge of the bed. "I'm getting out of here now."

"Jo, wait." She went to the table where the cake should have been, but instead a small, thin, rectangular black tablet was in its place. "Look. I brought this back for you. It's your diary."

I stood and my legs carried my body weight effortlessly as I grabbed the pocket-sized tablet from her hand. While staring down at it, the screen lit up. And the words, "Hello, Jovial!" Appeared onscreen as if awakening upon recognizing my face. I prompted it to open my diary with a click of my forefinger and swiped through the pages until the name Ian in a fancy font stopped me.

"Today's the day me and Ian will go through with it. We can't sit around waiting for someone to stop us, because I know they will. We have to make a move and do this now. Hopefully, it all goes as planned and we could be free of the hellhole."

After reading the passage, I looked up into her wide, round eyes and instinct made it clear that she was not to be trusted. Something about the diary threw me off. I held the tablet in my palms and examined it, front and back, hoping it would settle into my grip the way it had when I last used it and spark a memory of Ian, our motive, or provide some details I was lacking. The diary only proved to be another source of frustration and anger. Yet I slipped it into the breast pocket of my hospital gown, pleased to have the physical representation of me and my memories back in my possession.

The beeping from the machine increased, stealing my attention. The only thing running through my mind as a memory was that machine transforming and gripping my wrists. Somehow that computer was linked to the lock on the door. And by the way Mom was watching me, standing guard over me like a vulture, I knew she wouldn't willingly be of help.

She was keeping the truth from me, hiding secrets, and doing things behind my back when she thought I wasn't aware. There was no doubting that now. And in my eyes, those weren't the characteristics of a loving, caring mother.

I needed that door to open. I needed to get out of this room. And the only chance I would have to accomplish that was to bring Dr. Schwartz back in.

I patted my breast pocket for emphasis. "You'd bring my diary but not Ian?" One thing I knew for sure was that if I had kept a diary, I would have hidden it from prying eyes, especially hers. This tablet seemed to be easily accessible to her and that worried me.

But of course, she had an answer for everything. "His caregivers wouldn't allow him to come."

"He didn't send a message?" I shook my head in confusion. "Did he even ask about me or wonder how I am doing?" Looking back over my recent memories, it was her who brought him up. She wanted me to remember him. And now that he was the topic of discussion, she didn't have any answers.

And curiously the answers she did have seemed to derive from my diary, as I recalled her first mention of it after mentioning his name. "He was your boyfriend. Or at least it was thought he was. You never told me about him, but then again you never really told me anything. You mentioned him in your diary though."

"He—" she stuttered.

I lunged forward, grabbing her by the shoulders and digging my fingers into her flesh. "You're lying to me, aren't you?"

"No, let go of me, Jo." She gasped and twisted, trying to break free of my grip. "You need to calm down. You're hurting me."

I allowed my anger to boil, refusing to prevent my emotions from influencing my actions as she's been desperately trying to discourage. The beeping on the monitor increased, but I blocked it out, focusing on her quivering lips. Without a second thought, I shook her and demanded, "Open the door," through clenched teeth.

"I can't do that." The fear in her eyes caused tears to hover on the lids. "Only the doctor can open it. Now let me go."

"I saw you." How could she blatantly lie to me, but most importantly why? I dug my fingers into her flesh, feeling the bony layer beneath. She cried out in pain and I only stopped when I sensed the joint weaken and threaten to snap. "I saw you open the door and leave. Now, let me out."

The fear in her eyes nearly paralyzed me, but the feeling of having lived this moment before instantly washed over me. A vision of gripping her shoulders while demanding action from her entered my mind. In that memory, she screamed back, tears pouring down her face. "Jovial, stop!" she begged just like my memory. "You're hurting me."

I shook the memory out of my mind and released her as she slumped into a pile of sobbing mass on the floor. To find sympathy for her after exposing her lie proved difficult. And although a bit of remorse crept in, I shunned it away, refusing to let it settle.

Time for plan B. I marched to the computer and banged the monitor with my fists. "Wake up, you bastard. Open the door."

"Please step away from the equipment," it chimed in that nauseating robotic voice.

"Wake up, you piece of shit!" I pushed and yanked at the block of metal, trying my best to topple the machine or destroy it in some way. "Come on. What are you waiting for?"

"Your doctor will be in shortly."

The loud beeping increased, doubling in a few short seconds and matching the rate of my heart until it became difficult to distinguish the beeping from the blaring alarms. "Wake up! Wake up!" I demanded, pummeling the screen with the base of my fists.

Finally, the sound of the door clicking open behind me got my attention. Dr Schwartz stood in the doorway. "Ms. Spencer." His tone mismatched the chaos in the atmosphere as he exuded a nonchalant aura. "It would be wise of you not to damage that machine." He took one step over the threshold, entering the room, and the door slowly swung on its hinges, lessening the gap.

Before he could allow the door to completely close and lock, I sprinted toward him, putting all my faith in the regained strength of my legs.

"Stop!" he ordered, bracing himself, but the force of my body knocked him onto the floor. I used the momentum to tumble through the opening and out the door before he could say another word.

Finally, on the other side of the door, my feet carried me down a wide, pristine hall. I barely had enough time to take in the details of my surroundings before turning down another long corridor which led me further along sterile, white walls that radiated under the florescent ceiling lights.

"Ms. Spencer." Dr Schwartz's deep voice echoed from far behind. "It is imperative that you return to your room."

The halls were empty, and the walls were bare which resembled my private room he was urging me to return to. Not even a poster decorated the space. The only detail that stood out as I continued my sprint was the lack of physicians or personnel.

Surprised that my legs were as strong as they were and not giving up on me, I continued on refusing to look back.

Finally, able to turn a corner, I only paused when a row of doors lining the walls of the corridor greeted me. My first instinct was to enter one to hide. To find a place to tuck away just in case Dr. Schwartz, Mom or that damn monitor machine was on my tail.

I wouldn't allow them to bound and restrain me again. I couldn't let them sedate me for who knows how long or examine me for god knows what.

My fingertips touched the lever of the nearest door, surprisingly it turned. I pushed the door open with ease, slid inside the dimly lit room and closed it behind me. I listened to the sound of heavy footsteps and commotion outside of the door as the booted footfalls came and went.

My name echoed down the empty corridors as they exited from Mom's lips. "Jo? Please, Jo." She had been following me and by the sound of her voice, she was close.

Dr. Schwartz's particular deep and dispassionate tone followed her as they called one after the other, "Jovial? You must come back. It is in your best interest to return to your room."

"Yes, honey," Mom chimed. "We're just trying to help you. Please."

In trying to remain silent, I slowly backed away from the door and pivoted, getting a glimpse of the contents of the room. A dozen of identical computer monitors were arranged side by side in the center of the large space, their jumping green lines and numbers danced on the screens. I wanted to follow the cords and cables to assess where they led or what they were keeping track of but there weren't any visible. Were they being powered by some sort of battery?

The room was dark, besides the glow from the monitors and small lights above them that focused a soft beam toward the edge of the room. When I followed the beam, my eyes settled and adjusted. My jaw dropped, and I brought my hand to my mouth to capture my gasp.

Obscure in the shadows aligning the wall, were the unconscious bodies of a dozen males of various height, weight, skin tone, and age. Their naked bodies were arranged upright along each wall as if they were a decorative part of the room's aesthetic. Two large straps positioned over their chest and thighs secured them in place as they rested their uncovered posterior against a slab of metal that looked similar to a vertical bed, reminding me of the one I had initially awakened on.

Were these people also in deep sleep? Were the monitors calculating their stint and remotely keeping track of their vitals? One of the bodies, a tall dark man with large muscles and a slim waist convulsed before going still again, and one of the monitors beeped in conjunction, startling me.

Questions about who these people were and how they were being so closely monitored entered my mind. I moved closer to the computer with the most activity on screen. I attempted to read the numbers and lines and make sense out of what I suspected were heart rate, blood pressure, oxygen intake, and even breaths per minute.

An eeriness crept over me as Dr. Schwartz's voice radiated down the halls, along with the sounds of adjacent doors in the hall opening and closing.

I watched the slumbering man's subtle twitches and how they correlated with the spikes in numbers on the screen. They were definitely being monitored remotely, but how? Were they implanted with something that kept track of that information?

At that thought, I pressed my palm against my stomach anticipating another flutter.

As the commotion of footsteps, doors opening and closing, and the occasional shout of my name echoed outside of the room, my eyes scanned the other unconscious males aligning the walls and stopped on the smallest one. The boy who looked to be not a day older than ten years old.

~~~

How do you feel and what are your thoughts on the latest revelations?

8: Breach

I moved across the large, sterile room toward the bodies along the wall to closely examine them in the dim light. Each one rested with closed eyes as if they were in a peaceful sleep, however, subtle jerky movements said otherwise. Some would open and close their fists ever so slightly as if they were trying to manipulate objects. Others would move their mouths as if talking or chewing, and still others would grimace or frown as if feeling pain or other sensations.

What was this? Were their bodies and limbs acting out parts of a dream?

Mom had mentioned the doctors possibly experimenting with space and time and placing consciousness into different dimensions. Was their consciousness in some other existence while their bodies remained strapped to a metal slab like wall ornaments?

She also mentioned how the wealthy would take liberty in using this place like a babysitting service and sending kids to Deep Sleep for the slightest offense. Could she be right? Had this boy been sent to Deep Sleep for disobeying his parents and not cleaning his room? Were all Deep Sleep patients being subjected to experiments involving alternate realities? Like the males, am I still sleeping and everything playing out in front of me is some sort of dream?

What was real anymore and how could I tell the difference?

I pulled the diary from my pocket and flipped through the electronic pages, the sounds of distant footsteps and the doors opening and closing outside of the room instilled me with a sense of urgency. As I swiped each page, scanning the lines for anything out of the ordinary, a passage finally caught my eye.

How can you prove whether at this moment we are sleeping, and all our thoughts are a dream; or whether we are awake, and talking to one another in the waking state?

As much as I wanted to concentrate on why I've come upon that particular phrase in my diary and ponder the chances of it being a coincidence, memories instantly flooded my mind at the full recollection of Plato's famous quote. Vivid images of Mom ramming her rigid forefinger into the center of my chest and shouting incoherent words, while a sense of anger accompanied the hatred in her eyes.

I continued to flick through the electronic pages, looking for anything else that could jog my memory.

Mom is acting weird again. Not only is she always running on booze, every time she gets wasted, she gets angry at me. She constantly stinks of liquor and I hate it. Just being around it gets under my skin. She keeps screaming at me about how I should be thankful because if she was in my shoes, she would do something different or better with her life... It's almost as if she wishes she were me.

Imagery of catching Mom in my room, sitting at my vanity, comb-ing the bristles of my brush through her hair swarmed me, causing my breath to hitch in my throat. When forcing my mind to continue the details of that scenario, I hit a blank wall.

However, another vivid picture played out in my mind instead. I questioned if it was a memory or my imagination that conjured up images of Ian's strong hands gracefully and sensually exploring my body and his warm lips on mine. The bitter taste of liquor and the strong stench that accompanied it lingered on my tongue, enhancing the physical sensation of his touch tenfold. His masculine scent of earthy raw almonds and the heat of his body radiated over me as we became more intimate and curious about the pleasures our bodies could produce.

My suspicions about Mom increased as the seconds went on, espe-cially after discovering how much I hated alcohol and its stench. Just how much of that intimate memory with Ian was real?

I stared at the small boy anchored against the wall with two wide durable cloth straps securing him in place. His small, delicate frame was made obvious in comparison to the fully developed male bodies on either side of him. But more apparent was the slight grimace that twisted his bruised lip.

Ideas and scenarios played inside my mind as I aimed to make sense of my predicament. I smacked my lips involuntarily, tasting the resid-ual acidic bitterness of alcohol from my memory. No matter what, I couldn't prevent my thoughts from considering how much of my intimate memory with Ian was someone else's memory altogether.

How farfetched would it be to not only remove someone's consciousness but to fill the void with another belonging to someone else? If I were truly sleeping during that year in Deep Sleep, was my mind the only part of me that slept? Were the rumors about experiments true, but instead of placing a person's consciousness in alternate realities they were being placed in alternate bodies?

My eyes were glued to the boy as I remembered Mom's words about the wealthy taking liberty in using the facility like a babysitting service. What if it were used as a form of entertainment or escapism as well? Those with older, fragile physiques implanted their conscious awareness in the bodies of their disobedient children for a thrill. When the bodies are no longer in use, they're returned to the facility for a tune-up before replacing the consciousnesses back into their rightful bodies.

Every year they come out with some new thing everyone wants to try or take advantage of, right? And for an experience like that, it made sense that the well-to-do would dish out large sums of money to jump at the unique opportunity.

The more I thought about the likelihood of that happening, the more I became convinced that someone had occupied my body during the year I was sleeping and took it for a test drive or even a joy ride. Someone who considered my body perfect, youthful, and had artistic abilities theirs would never possess. Someone who thought they would live life better and do things differently if they were me.

My breathing grew shallow and my temples ached at the thought. I took in a few deep breaths to prevent my panic from rising. Not sure if I were yet successful.

Of course, I wouldn't remember what was done with my body while my consciousness was removed, but maybe there was more to the flutter in my belly. Maybe those weird sensations held the key to the mystery.

Still, if Mom were to undergo such an undertaking, where would she acquire the amount of money it must have required to indulge in such an unethical method of escapism? If her story about why Ian and I ended up in treatment were true, it suggested we stole ten thousand dollars' worth of items because we didn't have money to legally obtain them. And what would we do with the items, sell them? Surely, if we were found guilty of the charge, they wouldn't allow us to keep the items or the money. In fact, we would've probably owed much more than we stole in court fees and fines alone.

Emotionally and mentally exhausted, my knees buckled under me at the thought and I gave in, dropping to the floor. My head ached. Tears distorted my vision and the impulse to cry out in frustration surged through me. For a split second, the urge to sleep prodded me, but I returned to my thoughts in order to push the need away.

As vivid as the scene was in my mind, a part of me wasn't sure if I had become intimate with Ian or if the person occupying my body did. How possible was it for me to awake with evidence of that intimacy growing in my body?

Was the thing inside of me a device that monitored my vitals ... or the beginnings of life?

I gripped my stomach out of instinct and a rapid beeping sounded from one of the rooms across the hall. It ceased immediately upon removing my hand.

Coincidence?

Again, I squeezed the flesh on my belly in the spot where the flutter had initially developed and the beeping rang out again, only stopping when I did.

I paused and listened, taking in my surroundings. Searching for the familiar sounds of nearby footsteps or voices. It was so eerily silent, an uneasy chill crept over me. Have Mom and Dr. Schwartz lost track of me? Were they in some other part of the facility or had they given up?

I crept to the door, nearly crawling on all fours to better gauge the safety of the perimeters. After silence took over the space and settled in, I placed my hand on the door handle and turned it ever so slowly to prevent even the slightest creak or groan from disturbing the peace. Finally, I eased the door open to peer through the crack.

Using my newfound beacon, I pressed my fingers deeper into the layer of flesh and muscles of my belly and the beeping chimed for a couple beats in the opposite room. Wherever the chiming was coming from, that was my destination.

I carefully stepped out into the empty hall, and tip toed my way down the polished tiles toward the door that housed the sound. With my hand on the knob, I turned the handle and to my surprise it too was unlocked. The door clicked when opening and only darkness peeked back at me through the crack.

Before I had a chance to step foot beyond the threshold and breach the entrance, footsteps at the end of the hall startled me. I leapt inside the room just as Dr. Schwartz in his immaculate white lab coat passed the corridor and continued onwards. He didn't even look down my hall as he walked by.

Before letting my guard down, my heart stopped when his deep voice called my name from the opposite end of the hall. I stood frozen, paralyzed by the logic. He passed the hall on the right, but his voice came from the left.

I inched the door closed with a click as bizarre thoughts bounced around in my mind. Maybe I wasn't as stable as I thought. Maybe Dr. Schwartz was on to something by keeping me here to address what had broken in my mind.

I couldn't trust my thoughts or memories let alone my very eyes.

After bolting the door lock, I pivoted in the darkness and the vastness of the room sucked me in. My eyes immediately looked beyond the similar arrangement of computer monitors in the center of the space in order to focus on the set of nude female bodies aligning the walls.

Stunned by the imagery, my hands went to my mouth to filter my gasp. Initially, instinct told me to search every nook and cranny for a familiar face, but as my eyes went from one person to the other, nothing in particular stood out. Like the men in the other room, the women varied in appearance, size and shape. And upon closer examination most of them seemed to make similar jerky movements or just lie motionless with only their chest rising and falling with their breaths.

Not a slab was unoccupied. And I questioned if I was ever one of the human ornaments that decorated these walls. Pity rose in my chest as I envisioned myself on the wall. Anyone could walk in and observe what these people probably expected would be private. Even so, no evidence of staff or personnel other than Dr. Schwartz was present in the facility.

Which concerned me on a completely other level.

Where were the personnel to keep him in check and to make sure his practices were meeting standards and remaining lawful? I've roamed many halls and a couple rooms with no security camera in sight. Was anyone keeping records of what was being done to these people?

Were there records on what has been done to me?

~~~

Only 2-3 more chapters until the end. In the meantime, please share your thoughts and theories!

9: Under Pressure

U pon pressing my fingers into the soft flesh of my gut, the center monitor beeped in conjunction. I ignored the throbbing discomfort to stand before it to see more numbers and lines dance onscreen. Not satisfied, I tapped the display to prompt it to change or demonstrate new information.

Nothing occurred as expected.

Again, my fingers pressed deeper creating a fleshy dent in my gut and the beeping commenced. A series of numbers appeared at the top of the screen and continually increased and decreased in amount as if counting or calculating. My belly ached as I squeezed harder, causing my breathing to become shallow.

Confused and overwhelmed, I gave up. My eyes scanned the room in a determined effort to absorb any information that could help me stitch together the intricate puzzle. With an unsatisfactory huff, I swiped through my diary again, this time skipping to the end to read the last entry dated a year ago.

I have to do this for Ian. He would want me to, I know he's counting on me. I can't just sit back and pretend—

The paragraph ended, and no more pages remained after that strange and abrupt phrase. What was I about to write? And more importantly, what did I need to do for Ian?

Suddenly it occurred to me that maybe I had written something important or significant, but someone deleted it. How could I even be sure the diary was truly mine or that I had written those words? There were so many questions and it was difficult to trust anyone with the correct answers.

Without access to a reliable clock, the sense of urgency hovered in the atmosphere as minutes seemed to move by in seconds. I rummaged through the small metal drawers beneath the machines. Not all of them opened, but the ones that were unlocked contained various sterile instruments in clear plastic packaging. Most of the equipment I didn't recognize, but I assumed they were medical and surgical tools judging by the sleek and smooth metal.

Finding nothing of use, I closed the drawers.

How do I get out of this hospital and where will I go once I leave?

Before turning away from the monitor, I caught a glimpse of my reflection on the screen. The same dark ringlets that spooled from Ian's fingertips framed my face. The distinct outline of my nose showed upon examining my profile, and memories of pressing the tips of my nose against Ian's flooded me.

I wanted to go home. I didn't know where home was or what waited for me, but I had to get there.

A hot tear crept down my cheek and I swiped it away, not willing to give in to my frustrations. Obviously, being in this room wasn't much help. I had to find the facility's exit.

Cautiously, I made my way back to the door and said a silent farewell to the sleeping women arranged on the wall behind me. I pressed my ear to the steal door, listening for any signs of life out in the hall. Satisfied, I turned the knob and pulled the door open to step out.

With soft steps, I moved slowly down the path of cold tiles back toward the way I came. Upon entering the adjacent hall, I stopped in my tracks to see Mom standing in the center with tears running down her reddened cheeks.

"Please, Jo." Her pleas came out above a whisper. "Don't do this." Some patches of hair clumped together near her temples and her unkempt appearance nearly made me sympathize as I understood the exhaustion she must have felt. Nonetheless, I was on a mission and nothing or no one would stop me.

I took a step back. Retreating backwards to put a decent amount of space between us, I kept my eyes glued to hers. As she pleaded with her fatigued gaze, I shook my head to portray my intent and turned to sprint, only to smack face first into Dr. Schwartz's chest. His gangly arms quickly captured me in a tight bear hug.

"Do not fight the inevitable." His monotone voice sent chills down my spine. "We need your cooperation if you want this to be successful."

I struggled against his grip, pulling, twisting, and turning in his arms. "I'm getting out of here. So, let me go. You can't hold me against my will."

Not even did his teeth grit during the struggle. "Ms. Spencer, it looks like I have failed with this one. It may be best to terminate—"

"No!" Mom cried out. "Please, doctor. We have to keep trying. This is important for me, for her ... for you. Please, we have to make this work."

"All signs are pointing to failure." He spoke as if I weren't there, as if he wasn't gripping me in his arms. "There is extensive damage, and even after everything I have attempted, she is not making progress. We must conclude this experiment."

As he held onto me with my arms tucked at my sides—reminding me of being strapped in bed upon waking, and the dozens of naked bodies strapped to the walls on display—I repeated his last words aloud. "Experiment?" I relaxed in his grip and stared into Mom's tear-filled eyes looking for an explanation.

"I'm so sorry, Jo. I'm so sorry, please forgive me." She pressed her palms together and the emotional pain that surged through her revealed itself in her body language. The way she slumped over as if carrying a heavy weight in her shoulder said volumes.

"What's going on?" Shock and anger escaped through my voice. "You allowed him to experiment on me? What did you do?" Anger rattled in my throat as I growled in her direction. "What did he do to me?"

"Dr. Schwartz offered me an opportunity I couldn't refuse." She huffed, trying to get the words out. "He needed more successful subjects for a new Rebirthing treatment he was hoping to get started. If he could maintain over a seventy-five percent success rate, then the administration would greenlight the program. I couldn't refuse his offer."

"You lied to me! Why did I ever trust you?" Tears streamed down my cheeks.

"I had to, Jovial." Her voice cracked and quivered as it raised. "I was trying to save your life." She dropped to her knees so hard, I could feel the pain radiate in her joints. She clasped her hands together and looked up at Dr. Schwartz as she begged. "Please, Doctor. Please give her one more chance. I promise we will make this a success. I'm begging you."

"What did you let him do to me?" I demanded an explanation not only with words but in my angry stare. I anticipated her confession about inserting her awareness into my body while allowing my consciousness to transport into different realities, or some similar form of mental torture. "You were inside my body, weren't you? Did you use my body for your entertainment while I was supposed to be rehabilitated for stealing? Tell me the truth. You owe me that now. Tell me, did you sleep with Ian Rodgers?"

A look of utter shock swept across her face as her jaw dropped at the accusation. "Absolutely not." She shook her head and stared unblinking. "Ian was found guilty for grand theft and was ordered to complete the Deep Sleep treatment. The point of sentencing him was to remove the urge to steal from his mind. You waited for him to return. You even counted the days, counting them down for an entire year. And when he finally came home, you realized the treatment worked. They successfully wiped his urge, but they also accidentally wiped his entire memory."

"What?" I nearly gasped. "What are you saying?"

"He didn't recognize you. He couldn't remember anything, not even his own name. In fact, he couldn't even remember how to speak. His brain was totally wiped clean."

"You're lying." Even though she seemed sincere, I refused to believe anything coming out of her mouth.

"Aphasia." Dr. Schwartz announced. "Loss of ability to understand or express speech."

"That's right." She nodded. "He was diagnosed with aphasia caused by brain damage."

"Brain injury," the doctor corrected.

"You were angry, Jo," she went on. "You were angry at the system; you were angry at me. You thought I had somehow ratted him out and had him sentenced."

"What are you talking about?" I sneered. "I thought they found some stolen items in my possession and that's why I was sentenced to Deep Sleep too."

"No, that was just a lie I made up because I didn't want to tell you the truth." She sniffed. "The truth is ..." She gulped. "You wanted revenge on the doctor, and you knew the only way to get close to him was to also be sentenced to Deep Sleep."

"Lies." I scowled. "I don't believe you."

"So, while I was in the bath one night." Her voice hitched. "You came in and attacked me." Her sobs were so heavy she could barely get through the rest of her sentence. "You attacked me, and I fought back. I did the most horrible thing."

I shook my head, seeing how emotionally and physically exhausted she appeared. "What did you do?"

"What do you remember?" She watched me through tear glistened eyes. "You gotta remember, Jo. You have to show Dr. Schwartz you remember. If your memory comes back, then you would be the success we're all hoping for. Because of that, I can't tell you everything. You have to do it on your own and remember."

I stared into her eyes, watching the tears spill over the lids like a rampant waterfall, shimmering and pulling me in like a crystal ball.

I searched my memory, allowing my thoughts to transport me back into the candle lit bathroom where I stood over Mom who was soaking in a bath full of fluffy white bubbles. She was humming a familiar tune, one that I couldn't recall the name of but was familiar, nonetheless.

Her head rested back against the rim of the rusted fiberglass tub and her eyes were closed. A look of peace and tranquility on her face.

I have to do this. I have to do this tonight, or my only chance is shot. I will just scare her enough for her to call the authorities and suggest I need treatment. But my reason needs to be convincing. It has to seem like I need to be treated to stop me from doing it again. This is for you, Ian.

With Mom's neck exposed, my fingers went around it. Her eyes snapped open and her mouth went wide as she gripped my hands to keep them from cutting off her ability to breathe. But as she tried to no avail, she kicked instead. Warm, soapy water spilt over the edge of the tub and onto my pants and shoes as I screamed, "It's your fault, isn't it? You reported Ian to those pigs, didn't you? He was only trying to feed and support his family. He has a good heart. How could you?"

"Stop—" She kicked and thrust her body, but I held on tight. "You're— hurting me."

"It's your fault, isn't it?" The fear in her eyes hurt my heart, but it was the busted blood vessel in her right eye that told me I had went too far. I immediately let go, gasping at the audacity I had to do what I just did. Images of Ian flooded my mind and I reminded myself the lengths I would go through to right the wrongs of a broken system. A system that would allow the brutal experimentation of society's youth, no matter the consequence.

Before I could back away, wet hands suddenly gripped my shirt and I plunged headfirst into the tub, hitting my head on the porcelain edge. Water rushed into my nose and mouth as I tried to catch a breath to protest, but the hands prevented me from getting up. Only the sad and fearful eyes stared back at me through the rippling distortion of the water until the snowy white foam sealed off my vision.

Snapping out of the memory, I stared into those same sad and fearful eyes. Shocked and in disbelief I let the words roll off of my tongue in bewilderment. "You drowned me." If my memories were correct, that was the last I recalled. "You held me under the water. You held me there until I stopped breathing."

"I'm so sorry, Jo. Believe me I am so sorry." She cried so hard her body quaked with each sob. "I love you so much. I didn't mean to hurt you. I was just so scared."

"How did I get here?"

She gulped and her hands began to jitter. "There were so many rumors about the Deep Sleep facility. That's true, there were several conspiracy theories floating around. One of those theories was that the facility was conducting all sorts of experiments. So, I contacted Dr. Schwartz to help me. I'd pay any price. Any price. I'd help with anything he asked if he would just help me."

"Instead of taking me to a real hospital?" Suspicious, I narrowed my eyes.

"A medical facility would have pronounced you dead on arrival and wouldn't have revived you. To save their precious time, rooms and equipment. They wouldn't waste a minute, especially on us poor minorities. Have you forgotten how crazy it is out there?"

"Revive me?"

"Your heart had stopped, Jo." She cried again. "You were dead, and I killed you." She bowed, sobbing into a puddle of tears and snot.

"I don't understand." There was still so much I couldn't fathom about why I was here.

Dr. Schwartz smacked his lips. "Low and behold, Ms. Spencer approached me at the right time as I was in need of someone like you. So, I offered my services as she gave me the ability to."

"What would you need me for? I turned my head to look beyond his glasses and into his dark, sunken eyes, taking note that his grip on me had become lax.

"The Rebirthing program."

Before he could completely finish his sentence, I interrupted him by jamming my elbow into his ribs and slipped from his grip. Mom called out, "No, Jo. Wait!" before I retreated down the hall and back into the room with the women arranged on display.

I locked the door and immediately went to the unlocked drawer of surgical equipment and retrieved the sharpest object I could find. A long, thin metal rod with a wider handle that resembled an ice pick. What a doctor would use an instrument like that for, I didn't know, however I was going to use it in my defense.

The door lever jiggled with resistance before effortlessly rotating. Just as Dr. Schwartz came into the room, I readjusted the weapon in my hand to get a better grip. I lifted it to make him fully aware of its presence. "Stay away from me. I'm warning you."

"You must see this plan of yours being futile, Miss Spencer." He stepped forward, his movement odd and unnaturally elegant. "There are many failsafe's in place to prevent you from harming me. Now, please put the instrument down."

"Jo?" Mom called from outside of the room. "You've done it. Can't you see? Your memory is coming back. We should be celebrating your success. You'll be talked about all over the news. You've done it!"

"Yes," Dr. Schwartz went on. "This is a cause for celebration. I'm sure you'll be the poster child of the new program. I'm also quite certain the government will compensate you fairly for your hardships."

"Screw you," I growled. "And screw this government." I lunged forward continuing my longwinded growl, and plunged the sharp, metal pick right into the center of his chest.

~~~

Two chapters Left! What are your thoughts on Jo's revelations?

10: Beyond Scrutiny

The look on Dr. Schwartz's face was that of contentment as red begin to ooze from the ice pick that pierced his chest. His dark, beady eyes locked on to mine, and I backed away when his hand encircled the handle of the instrument to yank it from his chest.

A splatter of hot red liquid misted my face. I jolted and retreated backwards until an object at my rear startled me. I had absentmindedly retreated into one of the poor, helpless women who remained asleep and strapped to the slab on the wall.

I eyed the drawer where the other surgical equipment lay, in preparation of the doctor's attack. But instead of rushing me or taking a step at all, he opened his mouth to say something and only a steady flow of viscous blood seeped from his thin lips before he collapsed to the floor.

He lay motionless as the puddle of red quickly spewed from his mouth and the hole in his chest to gather in a large puddle beneath him.

My heart raced as I eyed him in shock. I couldn't collect my thoughts let alone my emotions as pure disbelief and horror paralyzed me.

"Jo?" Mom called from beyond the door. "Please, Jo?"

I was about to step over him and run out the door until the alarm on one of the monitors blared, the way it had done in my room. The sirens were so loud, I placed my hands over my ears to dull the pain. Still, the shrieking alarms were disorienting as I backed into a corner to get my bearings and assess the room.

Within a few short seconds, the computer let out a hiss before the metal surrounding the machine released, twisted, twirled, coiled and shifted into a mockup of the machine that came alive in my room. The sound of metal clanking and bolts fastening echoed in the space as the alarms finally ceased. With wide eyes, I watched as the long metal arms extended from the body of the machine and it glided from its position between the other monitors to stand before Dr. Schwartz's lifeless body.

Would it attack me for attacking the doctor? Would it attempt to hold me in place until it notified authorities? My heart raced and my breathing became rapid at the thought.

It bent, flipped and shifted the mechanical parts of itself in order to grasp the doctor's body in its claws like hands and scoop him up to cradle him in its steel arms. Red continued to drip from Dr. Schwartz and on parts of the machine as it effortlessly carried his limp body toward the door. The door opened as if triggered by an invisible signal when the machine moved close, which allowed it passage through the door and out into the hall.

Mom's gasp crept in from the hall followed by a thud.

I picked up the bloodied ice pick and quickly exited the room to see Mom collapsed on the tiles near the door. I rushed to her side, seeing her chest rise and fall with her rapid breaths. She must've fainted from witnessing a life-sized machine carry Dr. Schwartz's dripping, lifeless body. Convinced that she would soon awaken, and determined to find a way out, I set my eyes on the machine as it turned the corner to disappeared down another hall.

With fear and uncertainty settling in my throat, and adrenaline and curiosity fueling me, I followed the machine and the sporadic drips of blood it left down the long hall into another, keeping a safe distance.

Although the machine had awakened, it didn't seem bothered by my presence. It was as if it had one duty and chose to fulfill that duty over any other.

Nearly tiptoeing down the brightly lit hall, being sure to avoid the drops of blood on the polished tiles, I kept my grip tight on my weapon and my sights on the machine as it rolled down the hall nearly silent. Being cautious of possible staff members or other machines, I quickly turned the hall to see the door to a room wide open. I spotted the clusters of red drips of red in the entryway that confirmed Dr. Schwartz was taken inside.

Ever so slowly, I crept forward, hearing commotion coming from the room and the sound of another door opening and closing inside.

As I was about to enter, the even, rhythmic sound of footsteps ahead of me froze me in place. Who else could be here? Since escaping from my room and roaming the halls there haven't been one sign of a person other than Mom and Dr. Schwartz.

For a second, curiosity kept me planted, but the door to the room slowly closing on its hinges urged me to move. No longer conflicted, I took a step toward the open door. The footsteps finally ceased at the end of the hall ahead of me as Dr. Schwartz pivoted around the corner like a silver-haired solider and paused.

I gasped, bringing my hand to my heart.

He wore his infamous, crisp white lab coat and thin rimmed glasses, yet neither was soiled or stained with blood. In fact, he gave off no sign that he had ever been injured. My damaged, fragile mind had to be playing tricks on me.

"Jovial—" he started, and I didn't stick around to listen. I ducked into the room and locked the door. I rested against the metal and waited for his footsteps to approach or the door lever to turn. After a few seconds of silence, I took in a relaxing breath before quickly turning to evaluate the space.

The room was bright and housed a large metal desk with several electronic tablets and a collection of menial odds and ends arranged on the top. Three large, flat screens stretched from one end of the desk to the other. The room had been set up like a medical doctor's office with a life-size plastic display of the skeletal system in one corner and a display of the organs of the human body in another.

In the back of the office was a closed door. I glanced at the base of the door where fresh red splotches stood out against the bright white tiles.

With my weapon still in hand, I made my way around to glance at the large monitors and better see what it was relaying onscreen.

My eyes widened as I focused in on the several small rectangular screens relaying videos it was capturing from a live surveillance system. The videos showed images of the rooms and halls. Some of the rooms I recognized, and one hall in particular caught my eyes as Mom remained unconscious on the tiles.

A realization hit me. All this time the doctor had been keeping video records. Curiously, I pressed the screen to switch between cameras. The cameras must've been well hidden because I haven't seen one since waking. Remembering Dr. Schwartz used the computer to order Mom to come to my room for our first visit upon initially waking. "Send Ms. Spencer back to room two-thirty-seven, please."

I found that room number and enlarged the video onscreen. The camera was angled directly in front of the now empty bed as if it were attached to the room's computer. I pressed a number and the image flipped to another angle, then pressed again to see yet another angle. Were there ten cameras in each of the rooms? Was he watching and aware of what was taking place this entire time?

I flipped through the cameras seeing hall after hall, and room after room, until I spotted what I was looking for. The exit. At the end of a hall, above a door was a red sign that announced it.

If he had video surveillance of the entire facility, why couldn't he find me when I escaped my room? With easy access to his computer, I clicked around searching for information that may spark a light on the murkiness. Finally, I opened a file labeled, "Rebirthing Program."

It opened up several more documents. I quickly skimmed the most recent files. Reading all my eyes could take in.

Subject does not have an urge to eat. Subject craved liquid refreshment only due to the damaged neurotransmitter at the base of the brain that resulted in a side effect of smelling burnt almonds.

Removing tissue from the cerebellum and severing nerves from the hippocampus are necessary in both the Deep Sleep treatment and the Rebirthing program, resulting in similar side effects. To prevent a common side effect of aphasia, subject's brain had been altered to include vocabulary, communication, and syntax boost. Probability of communication success: High. Recollection of memory is improving only with the assistance and prompting from subject's caretaker. Probability of successful recollection: Low.

Subject's implanted false memory involving being sentenced to the Deep Sleep program by the courts remains to be a firm belief in subject. To get subject to recollect true memories, subject will undergo the risky Recollection treatment. Subject will be permitted to physically act out her prior mission. Permission has been granted by subject's caretaker and the agreement officially signed.

I thought of Mom as I took in the last entry.

Subject's memory has not returned despite physician and caregiver's efforts. Termination of experiment is highly recommended.

Before I could let the information process, noise from the room behind me grabbed my attention. The sound of moving objects enhanced my curiosity. I left the monitors behind to creep toward the closed door behind me, positive that the machine and Dr. Schwartz were inside.

They had to be.

The figment outside was not real, it was a product of stress, exhaustion and whatever damage he had caused. Putting the ice pick in the doctor's chest was real. I felt every millimeter pierce every layer of skin, muscle and bone before settling in his heart.

I put my ear to the door before pushing it open and immediately stumbled back when the machine glided past as if not concerned with my presence. It maneuvered successfully around the large desk and security monitors and toward the door leading to the main hallway. The door opened by itself, and the machine continued on through as if returning to its original spot.

I feared who or what would walk in from the hall, so I quickly ran over to close and lock the door. Feeling a bit safer, I went back to the adjacent room to peer inside.

This time I couldn't hold back my scream or my panic. Arranged along the walls of the large room were dozens of bodies, just like the males and females in the other rooms. But this room particularly house several replicas of Dr. Schwartz all in the same white and crisp lab coat except for two.

One of the exceptions was strapped to the wall with an ice pick sized hole in his chest. The other was missing several fingers on one hand and still had a look of agony in his dark, beady eyes. Still, one space on the wall was vacant as the thick straps dangled at the sides of the unoccupied slab.

11: Rebirth Day

My feet carried me out of the room and down the halls, passed smeared droplets of blood on the once spotless tiles, and to Mom who remained unconscious on the ground. The route to the exit called me, but I couldn't continue on without her. Even when I tried to convince myself to move on alone, a tug at my heart kept me tethered me to her.

I tucked my weapon in my breast pocket alongside my diary and dropped to the floor beside her. "Mom?" I shook her shoulder. "Get up. Wake up. We gotta go."

She stirred, steadily regaining consciousness. "What?" When her eyes met mine, she screamed.

"Quiet." I instinctively placed my forefinger to my lips, taking a quick glimpse over my shoulder.

"Jo?" Her voice quivered. "What happened to you? Are you bleeding? Are you hurt?"

I looked down over my gown to the red platters and smears, I only imagined my face looking much worse. "I'm ok, but we have to go. Now."

She shook her head. "There's nowhere to go, Jo."

"The exit."

"It's locked and authorities are probably waiting at the door to lock us up." She looked down at the sporadic drips of blood that contrasted the overabundant white. "You've done it, huh? You killed Dr. Schwartz."

"No." My head shook so hard my temples ached. "There are others. Others just like him."

"What do you mean?" She squinted her eyes disbelievingly.

I glanced over my shoulder toward the direction of the surveillance room. "There are copies of him. Dozens. He's not the only one."

Mom's eyes went wide. "Oh, my god. That explains a lot."

"Let's go." I moved closer to slip my arms under hers to help her get off the floor.

"Put me down, Jo." She gently pushed me away. "We have to stay."

"Why?" I stood, watching her, judging her inaction as much as her actions. "For what? Because you signed a contract that gave him permission to experiment on me as a way to pay him back for reviving me?"

"You don't get it, do you?" She huffed and sniffed away the oncoming sobs that trembled her body. "You were dead, Jo. I didn't want to lose you."

I sneered, nearly speaking through clenched teeth. "Or maybe you didn't want to go down for murder. Maybe that was your reason for reviving me."

She gasped. "That's not true."

I dismissed her shock and stared toward the direction of the exit. "I want to go home."

"That urge to go home was implanted in your mind." She stared guiltily. "In order to keep you motivated to remember your true memories, the doctor implanted that urge. In theory, you would try harder to make progress with your treatment if going home was your goal. In truth, there's nothing to go home to."

"Why are you telling me this? Why now?"

"Because it's time for you to know the truth. And it's time for you to trust me." Her voice dropped down to a whisper. "The more determined you are to make this work, the better. We allowed you to escape. We allowed you to go in the rooms and see the others and access the notes. We did it all to help you remember your mission. Once you remember, then the treatment becomes a success."

"You knew about the people strapped to the walls, displayed like pretty decorations?" I glared.

"They're all part of the Rebirthing program, in various stages. But I had no idea Dr. Schwartz was a part of it too."

Were those replicas part of his fail-safes?

"So, I'm supposed to trust everything you're saying?"

"Yes. Because I'm telling you the truth." Her bottom lip quivered. "Remember when you were determined to become the best pianist in the district? It gave you purpose. Seeing the joy music brought you made living so much easier for us in that dump. I would go around the house humming all the beautiful songs you created. But when Ian came back damaged, you became determined for something else. Revenge." She nodded, encouragingly. "And that determination will heal you."

The memory of saying goodbye to Ian was the clearest of all recollections. It felt like more than a year ago. It marked the first and last time we would be together, intimately or otherwise. The warmth of his body replayed in my mind until it faded from my skin like a cold breeze. Even so, I knew one thing for sure. "When Ian left for Deep Sleep, I wrote every thought and fear about that place in my diary, including my fears that he wouldn't wake up from the treatment." The Plato quote flashed through my thoughts.

"Your diary ..." She inhaled, nodding as if building up courage. "I went through to erase any mention of Ian being in treatment, but I made sure to leave everything else untouched."

My eyes widened. "So, you did alter my diary."

"Only to bring you back to me." She squeezed the fabric at her chest in her fists. "I would do absolutely anything to bring you back and beg for your forgiveness. Anything."

The urge to go home overcame me, but I shrugged it off. A realization hit me in the center of my chest. "I'm damaged goods now." I would forever question what memories were true or implanted. "You always complained about raising me, why go through the trouble to revive me?" She could've left me at the bottom of the tub and went on with her life.

"Never." A stream of moisture dripped from her noise and she swiped it away with the back of her hand. "I may have turned to alcohol to help me get through the pain of raising a young woman on my own, but I never have and never will consider you damaged. I love you."

Suddenly, the overhead florescent lights went out and bright red light took its place, swamping the environment in a blood red hue. Wailing sirens rang out in the halls, startling us both.

"We have to go." Before my words could fully escape my lips, Dr. Schwartz appeared from around the corner. His unblemished lab coat only shone red due to the overhead lights.

"Surrender, Miss. Spencer." His deep, monotone voice was barely heard above the emergency sirens. "It's time to put an end to this."

I pulled the pick from my pocket and used all the anger, fear, and pain inside of me as fuel as I ran toward the doctor. I imagine slamming the pick far into his chest again, but he knocked me to the floor with a quick and unexpected jab to my ribs. Mom's screams matched the sirens as I struggled to stand and catch my breath at the same time.

The doctor straddled my body, quickly pinning back against the cold tiles with a firm grasp around my neck. He didn't utter a word and neither did I even though I tried. Neither a scream nor a breath managed to squeeze past my throat.

His fingers tightened around my neck and images of me and mom in the bathtub flashed before my mind. As the milliseconds ticked on, I became increasingly content with settling at the bottom of that bathtub. However, he anchored me back in reality when he stared unblinking into my eyes and announced, "Any second now."

His voice and the detached look in his eyes gave me the boost I craved to grip the pick in my hand tighter than he gripped my neck. I swung my arm and plunged the sharp metal into his temple, merely missing the ear canal. He collapsed over me, pinning me to the floor.

Before I could blink away the tears that accumulated in my vision, Mom's disheveled outline slowly came into view. She seemed exhausted from her failed attempts at preventing him from hurting me, in no time she was at my side helping me to stand. I took a few rapid breaths of relief when suddenly a sharp pain in my abdomen caused me to hunch over. "Oh no."

"Jo." Mom's eyes widened. "What's happening?"

"My stomach again." A wave of nausea hit me, and I nearly buckled from the pain. "What did he do to me?"

"He must be shutting it down." Her voice hitched in fear. "Oh, no. Our progress will be lost!"

I snapped my head to stare into her frightened eyes. "What are you saying? What's inside of me?"

She hesitated, staring at my hands that clenched my abdomen. "Those people you've seen in the rooms and Dr. Schwartz, they're not the only ones with synthetic bodies."

My jaw dropped. "No. What? I don't believe it." I doubled over in pain, dropping to my knees.

She knelt at my side. Worry in her face. "I had to, Jo. You were dead. Completely dead. You didn't think he just restarted your heart to revive you, right? That's not how rebirthing works. The only way to give you a new life was to transfer your awareness into a synthetic body. It cost so much and took so long, but if this program works, people will never die. We could just have them transferred to new bod—"

"No!" I screamed. Trying to process the thought of occupying a fully artificial body, of living in a body that wasn't completely my own but partly owned by someone else was unbearable. The violation and lack of control... "I'd rather die. Why didn't you just let me die?"

"I love you," her sobs caused her words to catch in her throat, "so much. I struggled to have you and raise you, but I would never give up on you. Ever."

The pain in my gut was excruciating, and I couldn't imagine what the doctor had done to cause so much agony. I screamed to relieve the pain while I yanked the ice pick from where I had planted it in Dr. Schwartz.

"Jo, Please." Mom stood and back away slowly with her hands up in front of her, showing she was no threat. "I'm so sorry, baby. I'm so sorry."

"I don't," I grunted as a wave of pain tore through me, "believe you."

"Everything I've confessed to you is true. Please."

My insides twisted and coiled as I raised the ice pick. Not a second thought entered my mind as I dove the sharp metal deep into the flesh of my belly, puncturing the spot where the pain was, and the fluttering used to be. The pain increased, but I wasn't satisfied until I could see what was happening inside of me with my very own eyes.

I yelled out in agony as the metal went in deeper, stopping only when it hit a hard object. Upon yanking the pick from my belly, a slim red wire with frayed strands of metal slid from the hole. "Oh, my god."

"Oh, no." Mom's hands went to her mouth.

I jerked the flexible cord, pulling out a long strand until it caught on something and dangled from my flesh. That wasn't enough. I had to see more. I ignore the surge of red liquid dribbling from the wound and mom's cries to plunge my fingers inside, exposing the turning and twisting mechanical parts alongside globs of gelatinous material.

My mouth hung open, but the scream was silent.

With surging fear, I looked up at Mom as a plea for help. She immediately rushed to my side, pressing her hand over the open wound to keep the spewing contents inside. "Don't worry. I'll find Dr. Schwartz and he'll fix you. Okay, I don't care if I have to sign over my life. He'll fix you and it'll be fine. Just fine."

"No." I shook my head, grimacing in pain and shock. "Just let me be. Let me die, already."

Her lips quivered as I slumped to the floor amongst the puddle of my own blood. "What about Ian, huh? You're gonna allow the government to win by not fighting for justice?"

I shook my head, feeling the life slowly drain out of me. "No, they will win if we succeed."

I welcomed the warm sensation of relief to swamp me and closed my eyes.

~~~

The sweet, earthy scent of almonds urged me to open my eyes. I glanced around the stark white room for the source of the smell, but my eyes landed on Mom instead. She was draped over the arm of the chair before me, her knees tucked under her as she slept.

The sweet smell reminded me of Ian's body scent and the first and last time we were intimate. I missed him. In the corner of the room on the table was a red cake with white frosting. Although this cake had several unused candles on the top, in white lettering it read: Happy Rebirthday, Jo. A slice was already cut from it, exposing its red center.

My mouth salivated at the thought of taking a bite, but a faint image of liquid red nearly caused me to vomit, and I lost my appetite instead.

I looked down at my neat and clean hospital gown, realizing I was secured to a hospital bed with thick durable straps around my chest and hips, keeping me from lifting my arms or walking out to freedom.

I turned my head, taking in the sights of the room. With the computer systems and large surgical equipment, the familiarity of the medical facility settled in.

I squirmed trying to free myself from the uncomfortable restraints, when a robotic voice emitted from the machine's speaker. "Please stay calm. Your doctor has been notified of your restlessness and will be in to assist you shortly."

Mom opened her eyes and immediately sat up. "Oh, my Jo." She approached the side of my bed. The closer she got the more I made out the abundance of grey hairs at her temples. Grays I hadn't seen before. The warmth of her voice embraced me before she did, and the smell of liquor wafted from her clothes as she held me in a one-sided hug. "Oh, look at you. Are you feeling okay? How's your memory?"

The monitor continued to beep, and I anticipated Dr. Schwartz entering the room, ready to ask questions and physically examine me.

I was prepared. More than ready. Determined.

As for the fate of the program, a thought popped into mind.

What a shame.

Lightning Source UK Ltd.
Milton Keynes UK
UKHW010638020123
414708UK00014B/755